Nutty's Christmas

by Claire Schumacher

William Morrow and Company New York 1984

1 2 3 4 5 6 7 8 9 10

Library of Congress Cataloging in Publication Data
Schumacher, Claire.   Nutty's Christmas. Summary: A squirrel accidentally gets into a tree that is cut down and taken away to be a family's Christmas tree. [1. Squirrels—Fiction.   2. Christmas—Fiction]
I. Title.   PZ7.S3914Nu   1984   [lEl]   83-26558
ISBN 0-688-03851-4
ISBN 0-688-03852-2 (lib. bdg.)

In a forest live a family of squirrels.
Father and Mother, Butty, Fluffy, Foxy and...

where is Nutty?

Nutty likes to climb trees looking for pinecones and nuts.
He has to hurry to catch up with his family.

Today Mother Squirrel is worried. "The woodcutters are in our forest," she warns the little squirrels. "Stay away from the pine trees, and no climbing.... Are you listening, Nutty? This means you, too!"

But Nutty has just spotted
a beautiful pinecone. *I'll just
hop up and take it,* thinks Nutty.

Nutty doesn't know that someone else
is looking at his tree.

Zzzz. Whrrr. Suddenly Nutty's tree is shaking all over. *What a big storm,* thinks Nutty.

The tree is falling down.
Nutty's eyes fill up with snow and tears.

Inside his tree, Nutty tells himself, "Mommy is going to come and get me in a second." But she doesn't.

Far away from his family, Nutty hears little voices calling, "Here it is! Here comes the Christmas tree!"

In the forest, Nutty's family is calling to him.

"Look," says Foxy, "Nutty's feet are printed in the snow."

"Oh, my dear little Nutty," sobs Mother Squirrel.

Nutty is still hidden deep inside
his tree. He is afraid to move.

Nutty sees little hands putting shiny balls and sparkling flowers on the branches.

"Hurry up, children, or we
will be late to pick up Grandma.
You, Brownie, stay outside
and guard the house."

As soon as the room is quiet, Nutty jumps out of the tree.

What funny flowers, thinks Nutty, tearing at the ribbons on the packages. They don't smell at all.

But a bottle of water smells like spring in the forest. Nutty opens up more packages and finds…

a car just his size.

Delicious smells
remind Nutty that
he hasn't eaten since
before the storm.

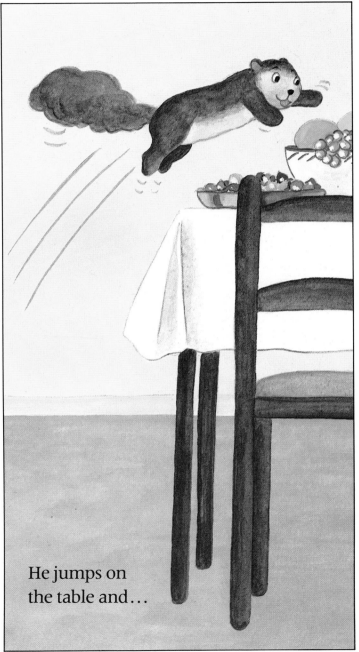

He jumps on
the table and...

tries a little bit of everything.

But a sudden noise
sends him scurrying
back to his tree.

"Who opened my packages?"
"Who tasted my cookies and
threw nutshells all over the floor?"

"What's wrong, Brownie?"

Poor Nutty!

It's a good thing the dollhouse window is too small for Brownie's nose.

"Now we know who made this mess," says Father. "Can we keep him?" beg the children. But Mother says, "We cannot let him spend Christmas lost and scared."

In the forest Nutty's family is still looking for him.
The truck frightens them, but imagine their surprise
when out jumps...

"Nutty, dear Nutty, it's so good to see you."

"It's good to be home."